POSTMAN PETE

written by Val Marshall and Bronwyn Tester
illustrated by Marjory Gardner

This edition first published in the United States of America in 1996
by **MONDO Publishing**

By arrangement with MULTIMEDIA INTERNATIONAL (UK) LTD

Printed in Hong Kong
First Mondo printing, February 1996
04 05 06 07 08 09   9 8 7 6 5

ISBN 1-57255-109-7

Originally published in Australia in 1988 by Horwitz Publications Pty Ltd
Original development by Robert Andersen & Associates and Snowball Educational

In Plympton lived a postman.
His name was Postman Pete.
He delivered the mail on his bike
To the people in the street.

And whether the day was hot or cold,
Through sun, or rain, or sleet,
The townsfolk knew they could rely
On good old Postman Pete.

An odd-shaped packet was in his bag
For Master Nicholas Sweet.
It was soft and funny, an Easter bunny?

No. A toy for his birthday treat!

TUESDAY

A letter was sent from Africa
For Mrs. Greenslade-Sledge.
It had a very unusual stamp
And stripes right'round the edge.

7

8

WEDNESDAY

A postcard came from far away
For Miss Priscilla Blunt.
It had a message on the back
And a photo on the front.

9

10

A cardboard tube was in the mail
For Ms. Teresa Trim.
It wasn't flat like an envelope,
But round like a rolling pin.

But one day Postman Pete delivered
To Miss Samantha Roy,
A gorgeous parcel tied with bows,
That made her jump for joy.

Pete still lives in Plympton
And brings the mail each day.
But now he's cool and comfortable,
As he goes upon his way.